EARLY BIRD STORIES™

Go Green
by Caring for Water

Lisa Bullard   illustrated by Xiao Xin

LERNER PUBLICATIONS ◆ MINNEAPOLIS

NOTE TO EDUCATORS

Find text recall questions at the end of each chapter. Critical-thinking and text feature questions are available on page 23. These help young readers learn to think critically about the topic by using the text, text features, and illustrations.

Lerner Publications Company
A division of Lerner Publishing Group, Inc.
241 First Avenue North
Minneapolis, MN 55401 USA

For reading levels and more information, look up this title at www.lernerbooks.com.

Photos on page 22 are used with the permission of: Ilya Akinshin/Shutterstock.com (sink); Ammit Jack/Shutterstock.com (dog); Jaros/Shutterstock.com (river).

Main body text set in Billy Infant 22/28.
Typeface provided by SparkyType.

Library of Congress Cataloging-in-Publication Data

Names: Bullard, Lisa, author. | Xin, Xiao, illustrator.
Title: Go green by caring for water / Lisa Bullard ; illustrated by Xiao Xin.
Description: Minneapolis : Lerner Publications, 2019. | Series: Go green (early bird stories) | Includes bibliographical references and index. | Audience: Age 5-8. | Audience: K to Grade 3.
Identifiers: LCCN 2018002890 (print) | LCCN 2017053541 (ebook) | ISBN 9781541524897 (eb pdf) | ISBN 9781541520172 (lb : alk. paper) | ISBN 9781541527119 (pb : alk. paper)
Subjects: LCSH: Water conservation—Juvenile literature. | Water-supply—Juvenile literature. | Water use—Juvenile literature.
Classification: LCC TD495 (print) | LCC TD495 .B85 2019 (ebook) | DDC 333.91/16—dc23
LC record available at https://lccn.loc.gov/2018002890

Manufactured in the United States of America
1-44353-34599-2/22/2018

TABLE OF CONTENTS

CHAPTER 1

MORE IMPORTANT THAN ROOT BEER

I'm working to be an Earth saver.

Earth has so much water!

I should learn more about water.

More than half of a human body is made of water.

Does that mean

we have fish inside?

Plants, animals, and people need water to live. People use water for more than just drinking.

We use water to grow food.

We use water to get clean.

It's even more important than root beer!

CHAPTER 2
STOP WATER WASTE

Most of Earth's water is salty.
Drinking it makes us sick.

Earth doesn't have much drinkable water.
So we can't waste it.

Even kids can conserve water. **Conserve** means "to not waste it."

A shower uses less water than a bath. Maybe I'll stay dirty to conserve water!

Why should people protect water?

Lots of water goes down the toilet. My family has a rule at home.

We say, "If it's pee, let it be."

How can you conserve water?

CHAPTER 3

KEEP WATER CLEAN

My dog, Daisy, goes to the bathroom outside. I don't want Daisy's dog doo-doo washing into the water underground.

I clean up after Daisy. Saving Earth can be smelly!

Litter often goes into lakes and rivers. This makes the water dirty.

Dirty water can make people sick.

Will you help me
conserve water?

And keep water clean?

Then I can find another way to save Earth tomorrow.

Water Saver

How does water get dirty?

LEARN ABOUT CARING FOR WATER

Some of the water we drink comes from underground. Other drinking water comes from lakes, streams, and rivers. This water is not salty like ocean water.

There are lots of ways to conserve water. Turn off the water while you brush your teeth. Do you wait until the shower water is hot before getting in? Catch the water in a pail while you wait. Use it to water plants or wash your dog.

New toilets use lots less water than old toilets. Maybe your family could save money for a new toilet? There are other ways to use less water in your toilet too. Ask a grown-up to look online.

You can buy special trash bags for pet cleanup. They break down more quickly than other bags. That means they are better for Earth.

Dirty water can make people sick. It is also bad for fish, animals, and plants. They can die if their water becomes too dirty.

THINK ABOUT CARING FOR WATER
CRITICAL-THINKING AND TEXT FEATURE QUESTIONS

How do people use water for fun?

How could dirty water become clean again?

What are the names of the chapters in this book?

How many pages are in this book?

GLOSSARY

conserve: to keep something from being wasted

drinkable: safe to drink

litter: trash that people leave lying around

protect: keep safe

TO LEARN MORE

BOOKS

Ball, Nate. *The Water Cycle.* New York: HarperCollins, 2017. Learn how dirty water becomes clean through the water cycle.

Spaight, Anne J. *Let's Explore Liquids.* Minneapolis: Lerner Publications, 2018. Find out more about Earth's most important liquid: water.

WEBSITE

National Geographic Kids: Earth Day
https://kids.nationalgeographic.com/explore/celebrations/earth-day/#earth-day-cleanup.jpg
This website has information about saving water, quizzes, and much more.

INDEX